This edition published by Parragon Books Ltd in 2013 and distributed by

Parragon Inc.
440 Park Avenue South, 13th Floor
New York, NY 10016
www.parragon.com

Copyright © 2013 Disney Enterprises, Inc.

Written & edited by Gillian Kirschner
Designed by Karl Tall
Production by Charlene Vaughan

ISBN 978-1-4723-2517-4

Printed in China

Ðɪsney

FROZEN

ANNA'S
BOOK OF SECRETS

PaRragon

Bath · New York · Singapore · Hong Kong · Cologne · Delhi
Melbourne · Amsterdam · Johannesburg · Shenzhen

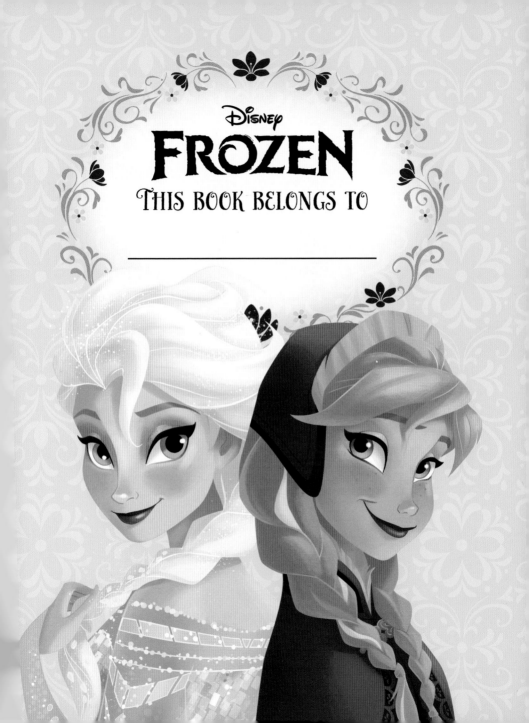

𝒟𝒾𝓈𝓃𝑒𝓎

FROZEN

THIS BOOK BELONGS TO

_____

All About Me

Anna wants to know everything about you! Write down all your details on these pages so you can keep it between you and Anna.

Name..

Nickname..

Birthday...

Hair color..

Eye color...

Address...

....

....

....

Email...

Phone..

Best friend...

Pets..

....

Family...

....

....

My best talent...

....

My worst habit..

....

My happiest memory...................................

....

....

Thing I am most proud of.........................

....

....

Secret Gallery

Create your very own special gallery of . . . you! Stick photos of yourself on these pages and keep them secretly stashed away.

Stick a photo of yourself here!

Me as a baby

Me on vacation

Me at home

Family Forever

Family is very important to Anna, especially when she realizes that she has a lot to learn about her sister. Make sure you find out all there is to know about your family and write it down on these pages.

Who makes you laugh the most?...

Who is best at helping you out?...

Who makes the most mess?...

Who gives the best hugs?...

How does your family describe you?

....

....

....

....

Stick your favorite family photograph here!

Sweet Dreams

Anna dreams of making new friends. What do you dream about? Keep your own secret dream diary!

Rate your dream

😊 for fun

😆 for scary

😁 for fun + scary!

Date ....
What my dream was about................................
....
....
Rating ....

Date ....
What my dream was about................................
....
....
Rating ....

Date ....

What my dream was about...

....

....

Rating ....

Date ....

What my dream was about...

....

....

Rating ....

Date ....

What my dream was about...

....

....

Rating ....

Story Time!

Anna loves adventure! Use these pages to tell Anna about a trip you've been on. Make sure you use lots of describing words to help paint a clear picture.

....

....

....

....

....

....

....

....

....

Amazing Adventures

Anna, Kristoff, Sven and Olaf set off on a chilly adventure to find Elsa. Would you like to go on an amazing adventure? Write about it here!

Where would you go?..

....

When would you go?..

....

How long would you go for?..

....

Who would you go with?..

....

....

....

....

Stuff to pack ....
....
....
....

Stuff to see ....
....
....
....

Stuff to do ....
....
....
....

Where In The World?

Stick pictures of your dream destinations and amazing adventure ideas on these pages.

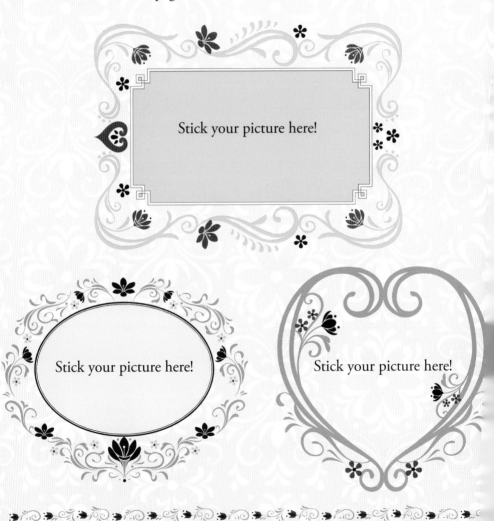

Stick your picture here!

Stick your picture here!

Stick your picture here!

Stick your
picture here!

Stick your picture here!

Stick your picture here!

Magical Memories!

Anna cherishes her memories of playing with her sister when she was little. Keep hold of your most treasured memories by creating a box filled with secrets and moments to remember.

How to make your memory box:

Grab a box—even an old shoebox will do! Fill it with things that you treasure and want to remember always. Then tuck it away in a safe place. Many years from now, you'll be glad you kept those things!

What is your first memory?

....

....

....

....

....

....

What item do you treasure the most and why?

....

....

....

....

....

....

Friends Lowdown

How well do you know your friends?
Fill in these details about your best
friends, then ask them for their answers
and see how well you did!

Stick their
picture here!

Name
....

What is their favorite movie?
....

Who makes them laugh the most?
....

What is their dream?
....
....
....

Name

....

What is their favorite movie?

....

Who makes them laugh the most?

....

What is their dream?

....

....

....

Stick their picture here!

Name

....

What is their favorite movie?

....

Who makes them laugh the most?

....

What is their dream?

....

....

....

Stick their
picture here!

Name

....
What is their favorite movie?

....
Who makes them laugh the most?

....
What is their dream?

....

....

....

Follow Your Heart

Would you follow your dreams, like Anna, or leave your heart behind?
Find out in this quiz. Check TRUE or FALSE for each statement, then look
at the results to reveal your destiny.

1. If my friends said my dream was silly, then I would give it up.
☐ TRUE
☐ FALSE

2. There are going to be too many challenges—I should think of
a new dream.
☐ TRUE
☐ FALSE

3. If it feels like my dream is a long way off,
then I'll stop pursuing it.
☐ TRUE
☐ FALSE

4. Everyone I know has the same dream. That's how I chose mine.
☐ TRUE
☐ FALSE

5. If I can't achieve my dream, then I'll just do something else.
☐ TRUE
☐ FALSE

If you answered . . .

Mostly **FALSE:**
Your dream is where your heart is. Congratulations, dreamer! It looks like nothing can stand between you and your dream. Just keep smiling through the tough times along the way, and you'll reach your destiny.

Mostly **TRUE:**
If you're willing to give up your dream because of what someone said, or because you aren't that sure about it, then maybe it isn't your dream. Don't worry, perhaps you just haven't found yours yet!

Sister Secrets

Anna's sister has been keeping a very big secret from her.
Can you keep a secret too? Write about them here.

What's the biggest secret you've ever shared?

....

....

....

Have you ever spilled someone else's secret? What was it?

....

....

....

Which secrets would you share with Anna?

....

....

....

What's the funniest secret you've ever kept from someone?

....

....

....

Be Anything You Want To Be!

Anna isn't sure what she wants to be when she grows up. It's never easy deciding what you want to be, so use these pages to help you figure it out.

Write about what you want to be when you grow up.

....

....

....

....

....

....

....

....

....

....

List five things that can help you be what you want to be!

1 ....

....

2 ....

....

3 ....

....

....

....

....

....

Sparkling Birthdays

To make sure that you remember the most important day of the year for your friends and family you can write everyone's birthdays here. Think of some princess gift ideas for each birthday, too!

Name ....

Birthday ....

Age this year ....

Gift ideas ....

....

Name ....

Birthday ....

Age this year ....

Gift ideas ....

....

Name ....

Birthday ....

Age this year ....

Gift ideas ....

....

Name ....

Birthday ....

Age this year ....

Gift ideas ....

....

Name ....

Birthday ....

Age this year ....

Gift ideas ....

....

Perfect Princess

Anna is the Princess of Arendelle—she lives in a majestic castle and wears beautiful dresses. If you were a princess what would you do every day, and what would you like to wear?

Princess name ....

....

Princess duties ....

....

If I were a princess I would ....

....

....

Describe your favorite royal dress!

....

....

....

Draw your perfect princess dress here!

Summer Fun And Snowy Hugs

Anna's snowy friend Olaf wants to hang out in the summer time and get warm hugs. What kind of things do you want to do with your friends in the summer? Fill in your wishes here.

....

....

....

....

....

....

....

....

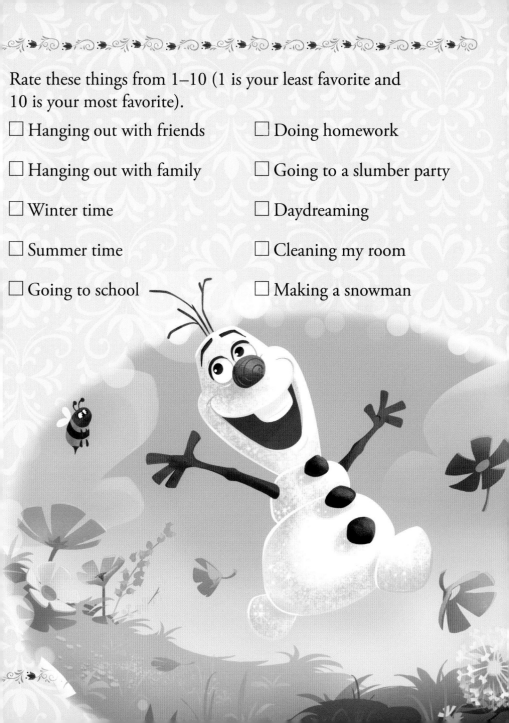

Rate these things from 1–10 (1 is your least favorite and 10 is your most favorite).

☐ Hanging out with friends

☐ Hanging out with family

☐ Winter time

☐ Summer time

☐ Going to school

☐ Doing homework

☐ Going to a slumber party

☐ Daydreaming

☐ Cleaning my room

☐ Making a snowman

Animal Friends

Sven is a comical reindeer and becomes one of Anna's closest friends. Do you have any animal friends? If you don't, fill in these pages for your dream pet.

Type of animal

....

Name

....

Age

....

Color

....

Favorite food

....

Favorite game

....

Best trick

....

I love my animal friend because . . .

....

....

....

....

Stick a photo of your animal friend here!

Summer Celebration

Anna wants to throw Olaf a summer-themed party so he can enjoy summer fun, but without the heat! Help her plan the party and write your ideas here.

Sunny-style drinks:

1 ....

2 ....

3 ....

Picnic snacks:

1 ....

2 ....

3 ....

Summer songs to sing:

1 ....

2 ....

3 ....

Tropical party games:

1 ....

2 ....

3 ....

How would you decorate your party?
Draw your idea for the party scene here:

Royal Quiz

Which of the royal sisters are you most like? Fun and happy Anna, or serious and sensible Elsa? Take this quiz to find out!

My favorite pastime would be:
A. Planning my next adventure.
B. Practicing my royal duties.

My ideal vacation would be:
A. A walking holiday in the summer.
B. Skiing in the snowy mountains.

My favorite outfit would be:
A. A colorful dress with lace-up boots.
B. A sparkling gown and cape the color of snow.

Which statement do you agree with the most?
A. I'm never allowed to do what I want to do.
B. I know what is right for everyone.

Perfect Princess or a Free Spirit?

If you answered mostly **As** . . . then you are most like the **LOVABLE ANNA**! Anna sees the best in everything and is always ready for an adventure. If you answered mostly **Bs** . . . then you are most like the **GRACEFUL ELSA**! Elsa is a great queen and is always in control.